TOTALLY TWISTED PUZZLES

Definitely NOT for Penguins!

Hi, I'm **PENGUIN.** Keep a look out for me as you work through this book!

You may have gathered that this is not a normal puzzle book. In fact, it's a **TOTALLY TWISTED** puzzle boo!

Some puzzles are easy and some are hard, but beware—things are not always what they seem! Keep your wits about you. You'll need all the wits you have!

This book is definitely not for penguins. Well, apart from me, but then I am **TOTALLY TWISTED** . . .

Before you start, check out the **TOP-SECRET CODE.** You'll need this for some of the puzzles. Why not use it with your friends to send each other top-secret messages, too?

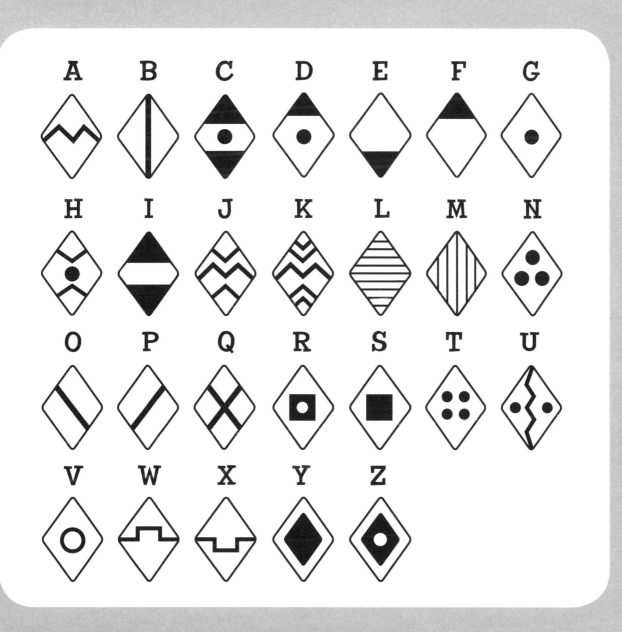

I'm a MASTERPIECE!

Draw your **portrait** below.

Your name in top-secret code is:

_____

Who would live in a **house** like this?

Draw the **home** of your dreams.

Make this half-monster a **whole monster.**

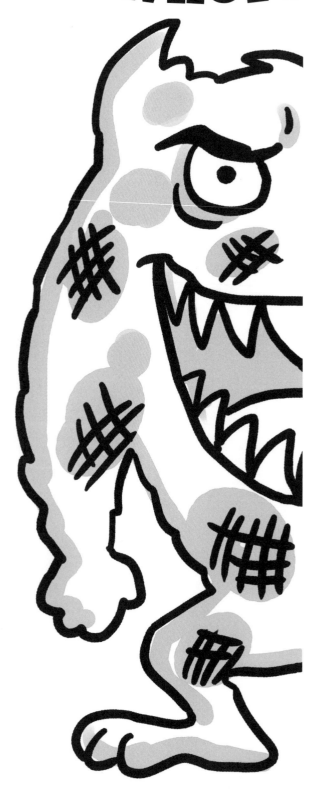

Draw the other half.

Give a name to each of these mixed-up **animals!**

_____   _____

_____   _____

How many **planets** can you **count?**

1

Stop! It's doodle time!
Draw the first thing that comes into your head....

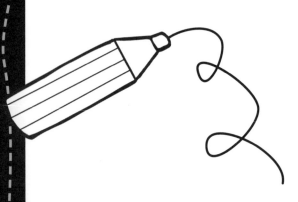

Penguins love to doodle!

How many **circles** are in this pattern?

2

Fill them in.

Can you connect the dots to draw a spotted DALMATIAN?

Match up the **fruit** and **vegetable** halves.

b

c

d

a

1

2

3

4

③

4 Finish these **patterns** by **drawing** what comes next.

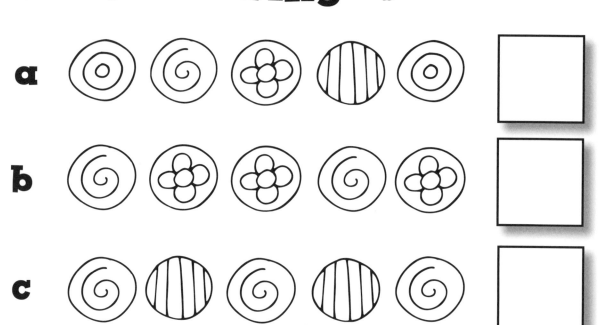

a

b

c

Spot the differences!

What are the **fish** and the **diver** afraid of? Draw it!

Time for a quick doodle!

Hurry up!

Tick! Tock!

Complete the **maze** to help the **wizard** find his **way** to the **castle.**

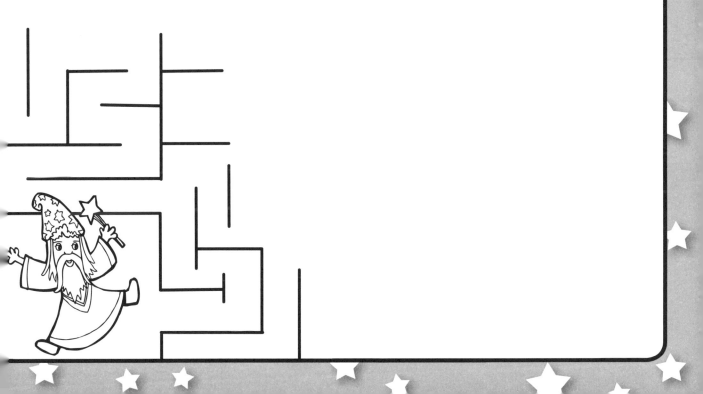

Match the **feet** to the correct **body.**

a

b

c

d

1

2

3

4

What has this **astronaut** discovered? **Draw** it!

Draw a picture of you and your family... as PiRaTES!

How many **pointy** teeth can you **count**?

8

DRAW what comes **NEXT** in these **PATTERNS.**

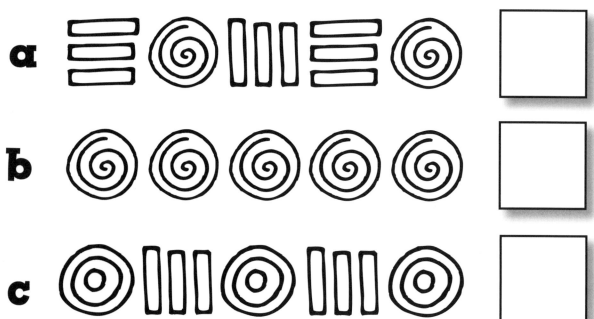

a

b

c

Complete this **picture** of a
magical **fairy**.

DoOdle a daydream!

Put these **pieces** in the correct order from **head** to **toe** to make a picture of an **ogre.**

10

Solve the top-Secret Code.

11

a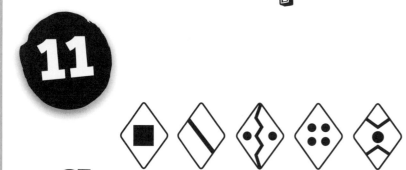

_____

b

_____

Learn some **facts** all about **me!**

c

_____

d

_____

Then use the words to Complete the **facts!**

Did you know?

a Penguins live at the _____ Pole.

b They can't ___.

c Penguins can ____.

d The _____ penguin is the biggest.

Which fact is not true?

DRAW the DRAGON

¡umop apisdn

What's **wrong** with this **pirate?**

Ahoy, matey!

12

13 Add the **missing** numbers to make each **total.**

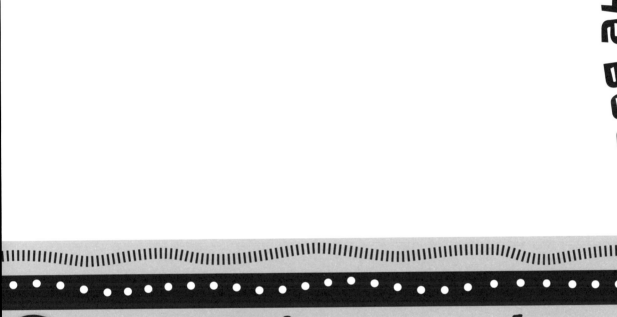

a) 10 − 5 + ◯ = **8**

b) 20 + 11 − ◯ = **21**

c) 3 − 13 + ◯ = **45**

Design yourself a **cool** coat of arms.

Each pattern and **symbol** should mean something to you.

Eek!

14

a b c d

Draw a **line** from the mouse to its matching **shadow**.

These **brain-boggling** puzzles are hard work! Take a **break.** **Draw** a d**oo**dle of p**oo**dle**s**!

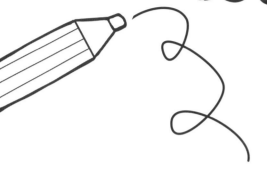

Look at these **two** pictures.
Look even **harder!**

15

How many **differences** can you **spot?**

DRAW the DINOSAUR the right WAY UP in the GRID below. COPY it square by SQUARE.

Roaaarrr!

These **happy** characters might look **normal.** Give each **one** a **totally** hilarious **name!**

_____

_____

_____

_____

_____

DRAW what comes **NEXT** in these **sequences.**

(a)

(b)

(c)

16

Here are four beans.

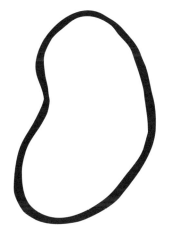

Runner bean

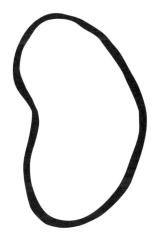

French bean

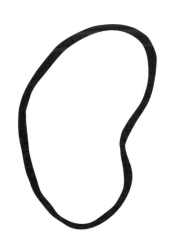

Mexican bean

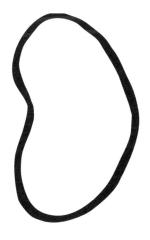

Jumping bean

Make them look like their names!

Your brain must be BAMBOOZLED from all those TWISTED PUZZLES

Take it easy and
doodle slooowwwlly...

17

What's wrong with this picture? Draw something in to make it right.

18

What's living on this ALIEN planet? Connect the DOTS to find out!

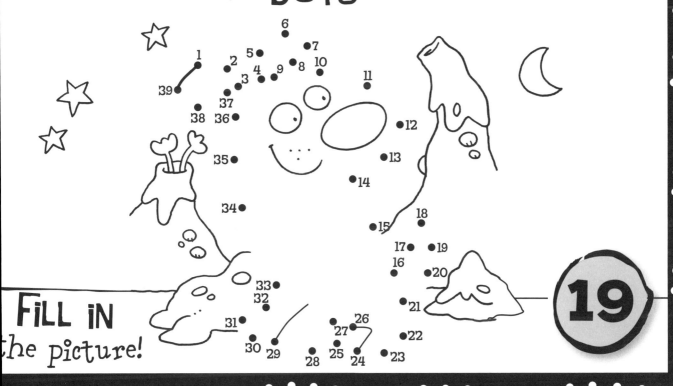

FILL IN the picture!

19

Draw lines to **match** the pairs of fluttering butterflies.

20

Fill this page with oodles of doodles made from noodles!

This doodle looks delicious!

The **leaves** have fallen from the **trees.** How many are on the **ground?**

22

Frogs love to play **hide** and **seek.**

23

Ribbit!

Ribbit!

How **many** can you find in this **scene?**

This girl is all mixed up!
Put the **pieces**
in the correct order
from **head** to **toe**.

a

b

c

d

e

f

Follow the lines to find out what foods these two aliens love.

Slurpster   Slimatron

What's for sale in this store?

Draw it in the window.

Draw a picture with your eyes **closed.** No peeking!

One bug, two bugs, three bugs, four...
Complete these sequences by drawing what comes next.

a **b** **c** **d** **e**

Time to TEST your MEMORY!
LOOk at these items for 60 SECONDS.

Now close your eyes and draw them on the opposite page.

How **many** did you **get?**

Draw yourself as a snowman

No **carrots** allowed!
Choose a different **vegetable**
for your **nose!**

This page is **TOTALLY TWISTED!**
Turn the book **upside down**.

27

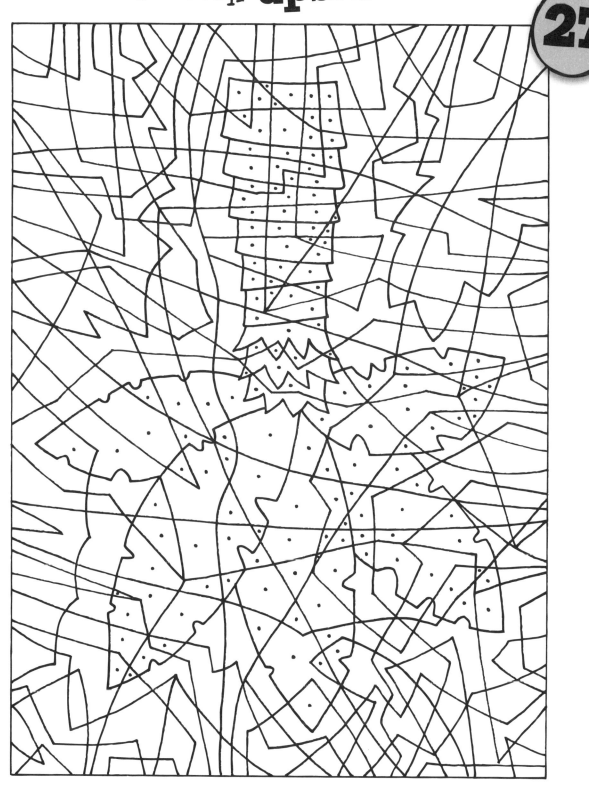

Shade the **shapes** that have **dots** in them.
What **picture** is revealed?

Draw some cool doodles between the CRACKS in the iCE.

No two **fairies** are ever the **same.** Can you **Spot** five differences between these two?

28

What's inside this PRESENT?

29

30

This knight is MISSING something very iMPORTANT.

What is it?

31

Write the **answers** to complete these **sums**.

21 ÷ 7 + 3 =

12 ÷ 4 × 10 =

Slugs love to talk . . . and talk and talk! Write or draw what these slimy pals are chatting about.

Night, night, **sleep** tight...
Find the **missing** piece to this puzzle **first!**

Here's a **trumpet.** Draw it on the **opposite page** ... using the hand you don't usually **draw** with!

Connect the dots to reveal this toothy creature!

Write a **warning** in the box!

Tick! Tock!

How many clocks?

33

This SPACE EXPLORER has landed on a strange planet. What did he FORGET?

34

Something has been SPILT on these pages
DOODLE around the shapes
to CREATE a picture.

Penguin has made FRONT PAGE NEWS!
But what has he been up to?
Write an ARTICLE.

Are you seeing **stars?** Draw what comes next in these **patterns.**

35

a

b

c

What do you think is in the **THIEF'S SACK?** Draw your **ANSWER** on the **RIGHT**.

Bug alert! Which piece completes each bug?

36

a

b

c

d

1

2

3

4

Put this **book** on the floor and trace your **foot**.

Don't **forget** to trace between your **toes!**

Name your **toes!**

Solve the top-secret Code to reveal the names of the fish.

a _____

b _____

c _____

This space explorer is all mixed up. Put the pieces in the correct order from head to toe.

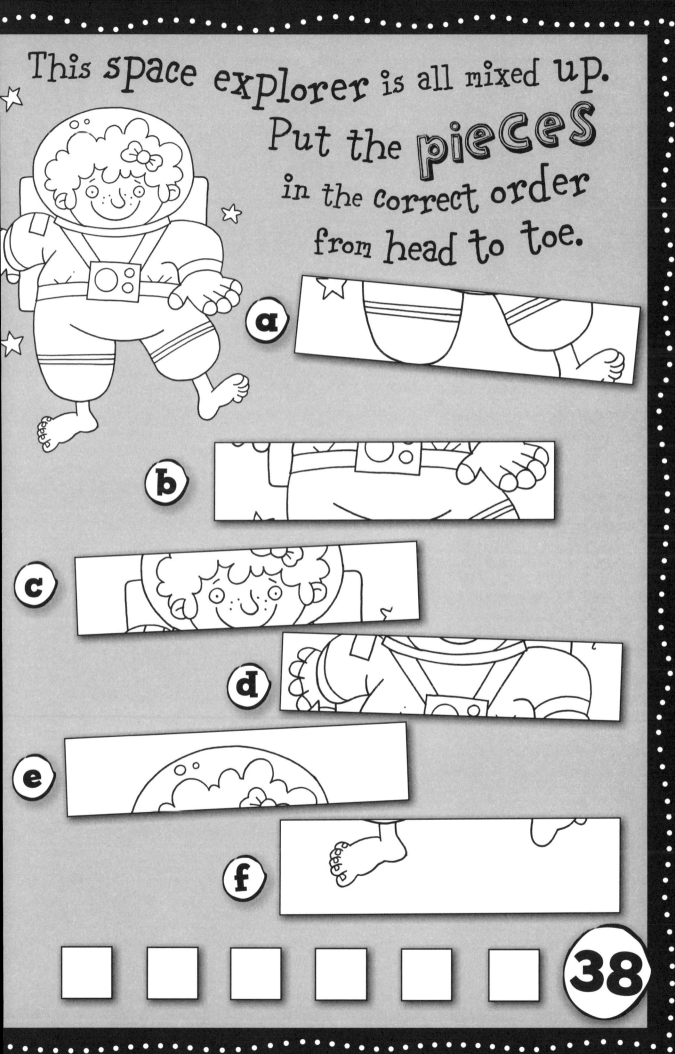

38

Draw a TOTALLY TWISTED doodle while Singing a Song you love.

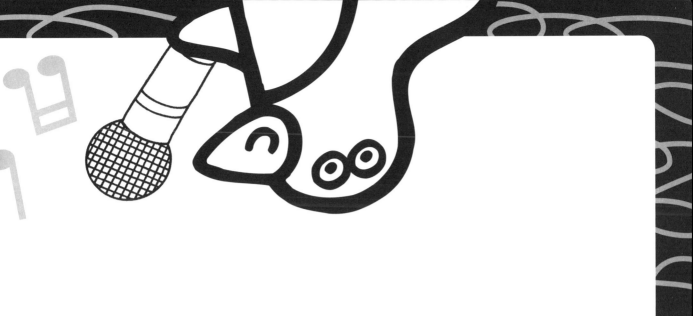

You sound like a rock star and draw like PICASSO!

Look at this crazy creature! Draw your own animal mash-up below!

How many candy canes can you find in this picture?

39

Draw an extraOrdinary hairstyle on this head.

Help the boy find his matching shadow. 40

How do these gremlins feel?
Draw their facial expressions.

This is the **last** doodle page in the **book.**
Make it a **good** one!

ANSWERS ❄

1 34 planets

2 127 circles

3 The pairs are: a3, b4, c1, and d2.

4 a b c

5 There are no differences!

6 a. Abraham Lincoln b. Florence Nightingale
c. Albert Einstein

7 The pairs are: a4, b1, c3,
and d2.

8 17 pointy teeth

9 a ||| b (spiral) c |||

10 The correct order is: c e b f d a.

11 a. South b. fly c. talk d. emperor
Fact c is false—penguins can't talk!

12 The pirate has two eye patches!

13 a. 3 b. 10 c. 55

14 Shadow a matches the mouse.

15 There are no differences!

16 a ☆ b 🌙 c ☆

17

18 The ball is missing!

19 A dog

20 The pairs are: ah, bi, cd, eg, and fj.

21 Piece d completes the picture.

22 36 leaves

23 12 frogs

24 The correct order is:
f b e d c a.

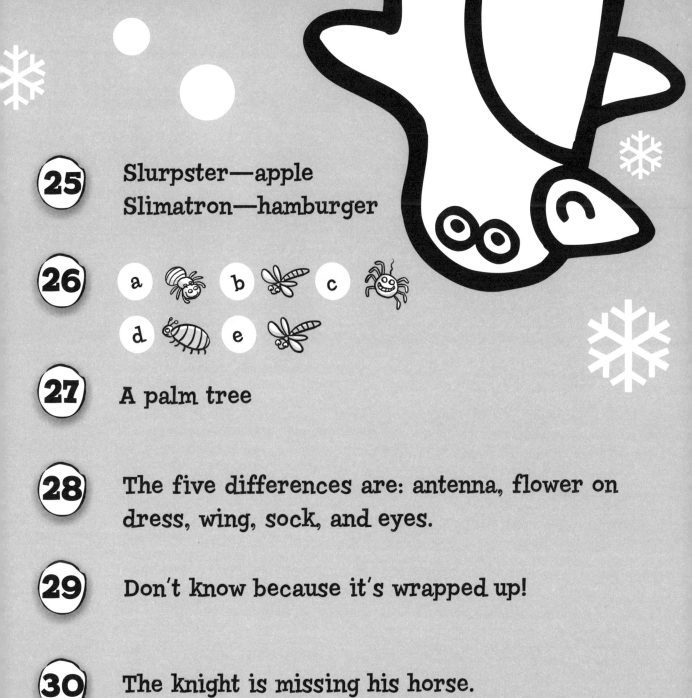

25 Slurpster—apple
Slimatron—hamburger

26 a b c
d e

27 A palm tree

28 The five differences are: antenna, flower on dress, wing, sock, and eyes.

29 Don't know because it's wrapped up!

30 The knight is missing his horse.

31 a. 6 b. 30

32 Piece e completes the picture.

33 19 clocks

34 He forgot his spacesuit!

35 a  b c

36 The pairs are: a4, b2, c1, and d3.

37 a. eel b. angelfish c. flounder

38 The correct order is: e c d b a f.

I hope you had a totally twisted! time!

39 12 candy canes

40 Shadow c matches the boy.